This Orchard
book belongs to

_____

_____

_____

ORCHARD BOOKS

96 Leonard Street, London, EC2A 4XD

Orchard Books Australia

32/45-51 Huntley Street, Alexandria, NSW 2015

ISBN 1 84362 845 7

First published in Great Britain in 1999

First published in paperback in 2000

This edition published in 2005

Text and illustrations © Adrian Reynolds 1999

The right of Adrian Reynolds to be identified as the author and illustrator

of this work has been asserted by him in accordance

with the Copyright, Designs and Patents Act, 1998.

A CIP catalogue record for this book is available from the British Library.

Printed in Hong Kong, China

1 3 5 7 9 10 8 6 4 2

Pete and Polo

Nursery Adventure

Adrian Reynolds

ORCHARD BOOKS

For Liz

"Wake up, Polo," said Pete. Today was their
first day at nursery school on their own –
without Mum this time. But Polo
thought he'd stay in bed.

At breakfast, Pete whispered to Polo,
"This is going to be our best adventure yet."

Polo wasn't so sure. "I don't think polar bears normally go to school," he said in a wobbly voice.

When they arrived at nursery school, there were lots
of Mums and Dads and children. It was very noisy.
All the other children had brought their teddy bears too.

Mrs Rose was waiting at the door to meet them.
"Hello, Pete," she said. "This is Henry. This is his first day at nursery school on his own too."

Mrs Rose took them inside and helped them hang up their coats and bags. Pete had his own special peg. So did Henry.

Pete took Polo out of his bag.

"Your bear's a funny colour," said Henry.
"Why isn't he brown like mine?"

"I'm not a funny colour," said Polo with a sniff.

"He's a polar bear," said Pete. "He's supposed
to be white."

"Follow me," said Mrs Rose as she led Pete and Polo into a big room full of children. It was full of bears too, but they were *all* brown. Pete squeezed Polo's paw very tightly.

Mrs Rose showed Pete and
Polo the painting corner . . .

. . . and then they built
towers out of building blocks.

They sailed boats
in the water . . .

. . . and then they
played dressing up.

There was even a pets corner. Pete fed the rabbit . . .

. . . and Polo fed
the goldfish.
"They're saying
hello to me," said
Polo feeling a bit
less sniffly.

Soon it was storytime. Mrs Rose read a story about a king and a queen and their pet dragon. Some of the other bears joined in, making loud growly dragon noises. Polo sat very quietly and very close to Pete.

Grrrr!

Grrrr!

Grrrr!

Grrrr!

Grrrr!

After the story, they had milk and apples.

Mrs Rose took some of the children to the toilet.
"Look, Polo," said Pete. "They're just
the right size for us." Then they washed their hands.

At playtime, all the children went outside, leaving their bears safely behind. Pete hoped Polo wouldn't be too lonely.

But he threw the ball around with the other children,
and together they all made lots of noise.

Soon it was time to go back inside – but at the door of the room all the children stopped still. There, in the corner, was an enormous pile of teddy bears. How would they ever be able to tell whose was whose?

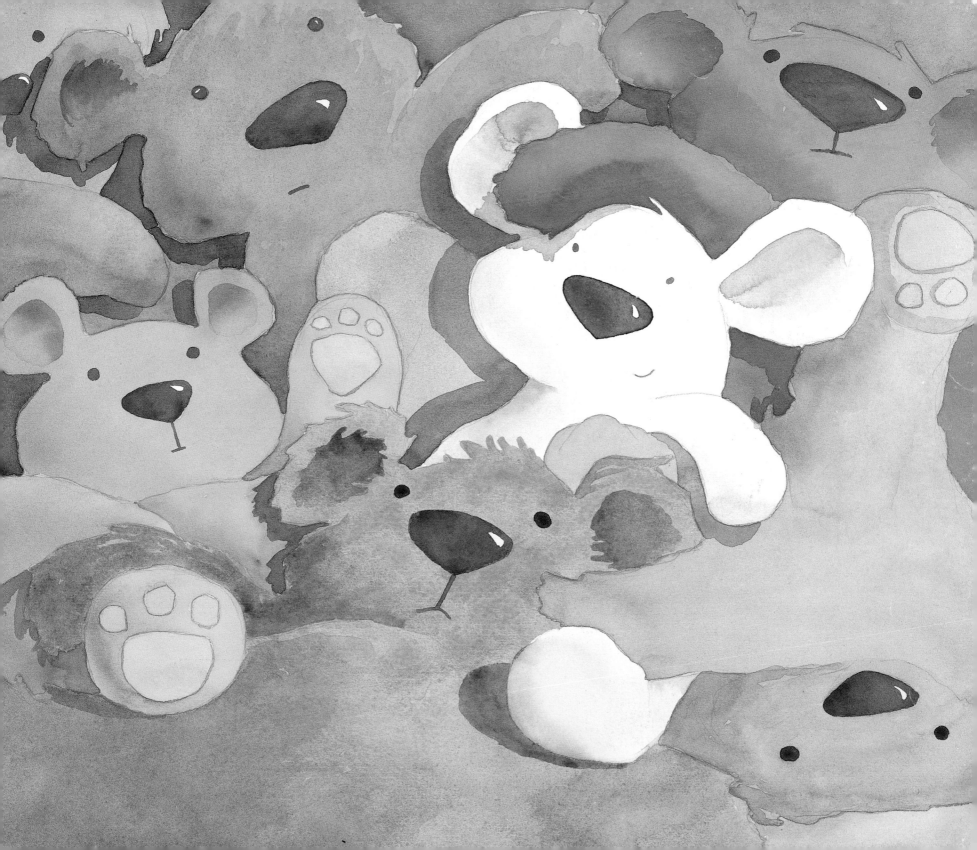

"Polo!" said Pete, spotting his own very special friend straightaway, and giving him a great big hug.

Polo was looking smiley for the first time all day.

"I had a lovely time with all the other bears," he said.

When nursery school was over, Pete and Polo rushed outside
to where Mum was waiting. They had so much to tell her . . .

. . . and they
both agreed that
going to nursery school
was their best adventure yet.